little bee books

An imprint of Bonnier Publishing Group

853 Broadway, New York, NY 10003

Copyright © 2014 by Georgie Birkett.

First published in Great Britain by Andersen Press.

This little bee books edition, 2015.

All rights reserved, including the right of reproduction in whole or in part in any form.

LITTLE BEE BOOKS is a trademark of Bonnier Publishing Group,

and associated colophon is a trademark of Bonnier Publishing Group.

Manufactured in Malaysia 06/15

First Edition 2 4 6 8 10 9 7 5 3 1

Library of Congress Control Number: 2015934158

ISBN 978-1-4998-0150-7

www.littlebeebooks.com

www.bonnierpublishing.com

TEDDY BEDTIME

Georgie Birkett

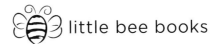
little bee books

Teddies play,
teddies jump,

teddies sing and
laugh....

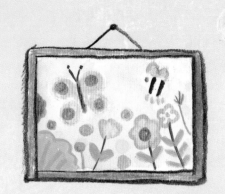

stairs...

the

up

going

Teddies

it's time to have a bath!

splashing teddies,

washing teddies,

teddies having fun!

Clean teddies,
　　dry teddies,

teddy pajamas on!

Time to brush your teeth,

and time to comb your hair.

Story time teddies

go almost . . . anywhere.

Cuddly teddies, snuggly teddies,

turning out the light.

Tired teddies, **sleepy**

teddies say "Goodnight."